Julie Downing

White Snow,
Blue Feather

BRADBURY PRESS   NEW YORK

To Barbara

Library of Congress Cataloging-in-Publication Data   Downing, Julie.   White snow, blue feather / by Julie Downing.   p.   cm.   Summary: While walking in the woods on a winter day, a little boy finds a blue feather and gives it to his mother. [1. Snow—Fiction. 2. Winter—Fiction. 3. Animals—Fiction.] I. Title. PZ7.D75928Wh 1989   [E]—dc19   89-815   CIP   AC   ISBN 0-02-732530-X

White snow everywhere.
Mom and I wonder if the birds
can find anything to eat.

Outside, the snow is icy cold

and deep.

I make a long blue trail
to the edge of the woods.

The wind whips snow in my face.
When I open my eyes I see pink,
yellow, and blue diamonds
dancing in the sun.

At the top of the hill, I stop.
Two golden deer are running by,
faster than I can ever go.

I scatter breadcrumbs and the
birds swoop down to eat them.
Redstarts and finches sing.
Blue jays caw.

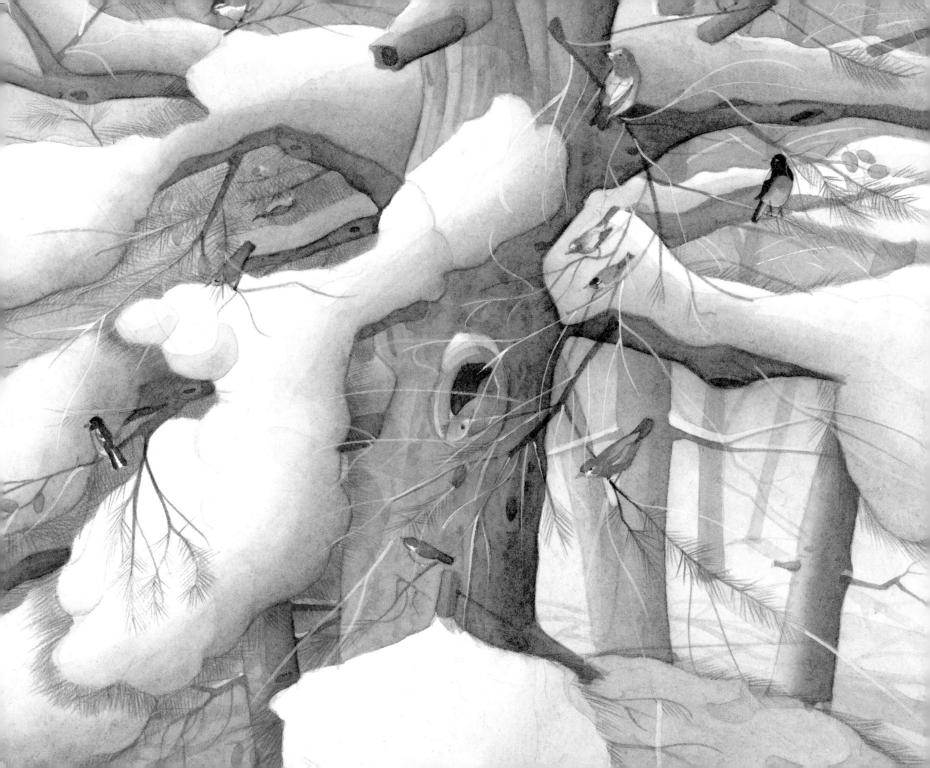

Underneath the tree,
I find sharp green needles
and fat brown cones.

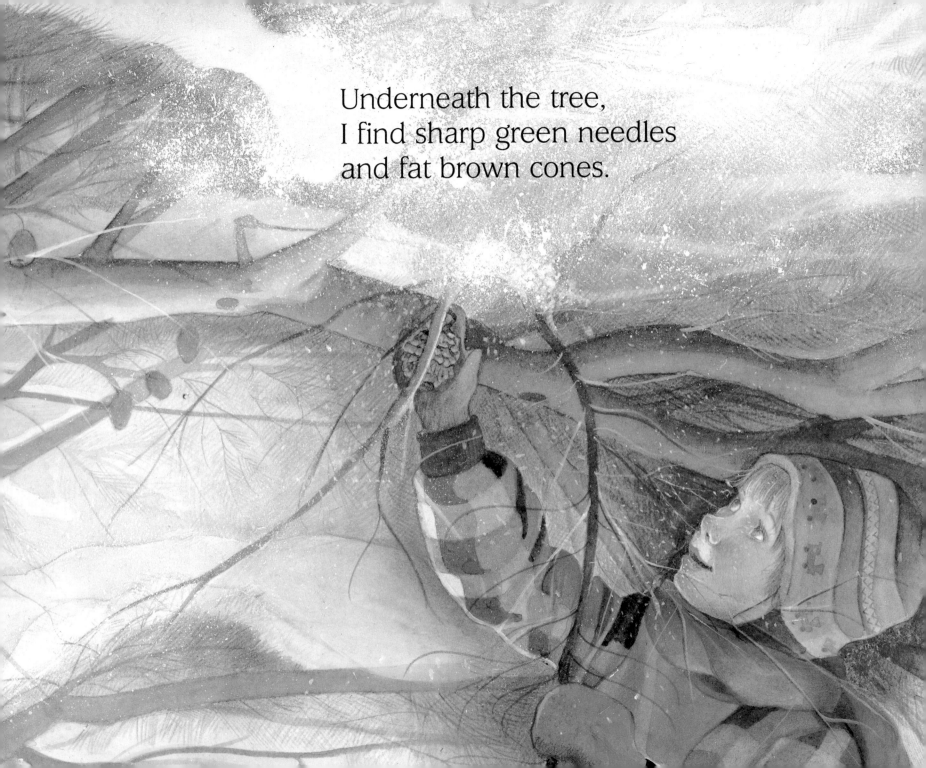

Ouch! My snow pillow prickles
with holly and red berries.

I chase a flash of pink—
a white rabbit, too quick to touch.

But I see a feather from a jay's wing.
It's as blue as the sky.

My shadow and I jump and slide
across the snow.

I found a piece of the sky.

And it's for you.